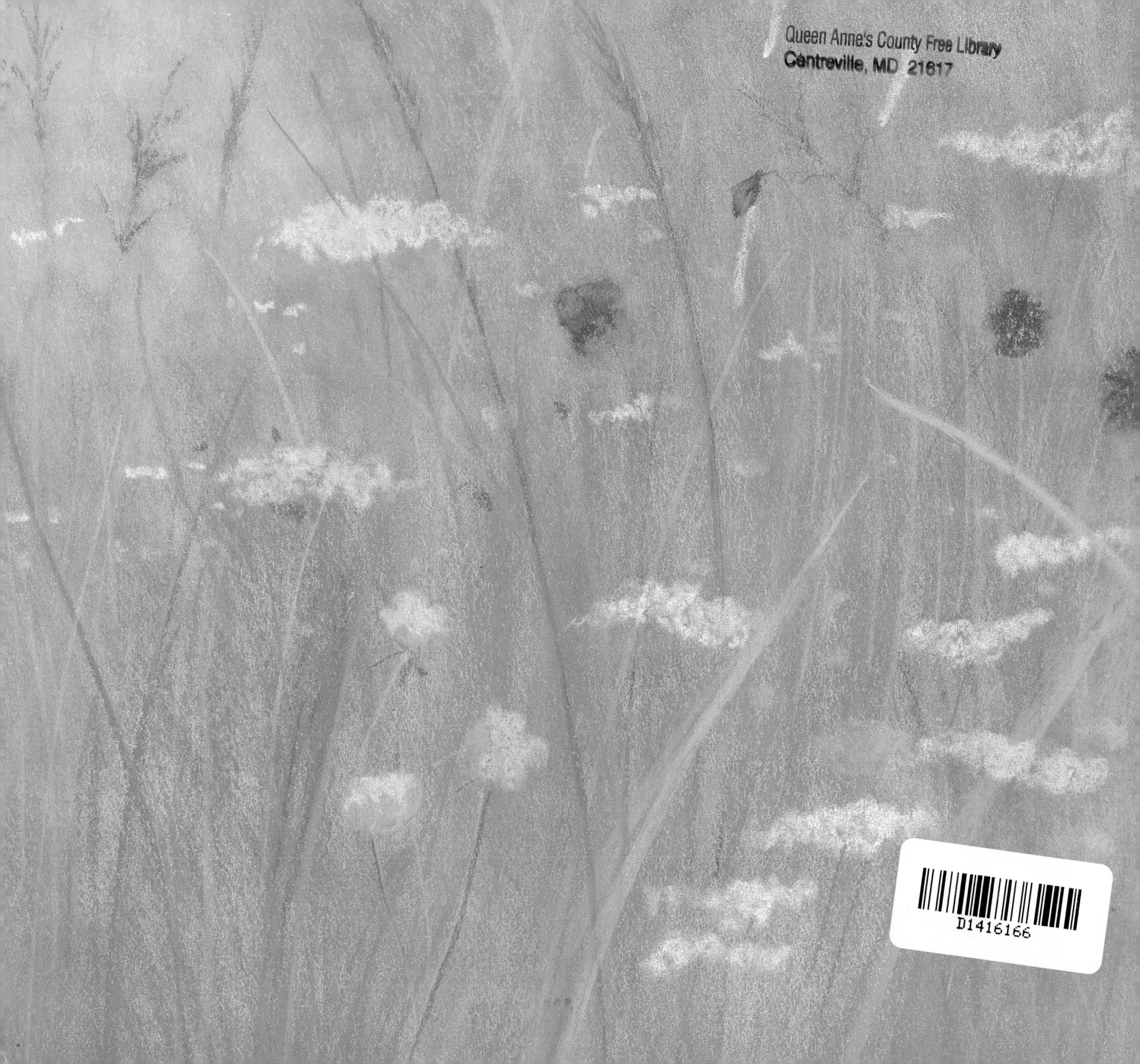

BW1   16.95   9/03

BLOOMSBURY
CHILDREN'S
BOOKS

Published by Bloomsbury, New York and London
Distributed to the trade by Holtzbrinck Publishers

Library of Congress Cataloging-in-Publication Data:
Hamilton, Richard.
Polly's picnic / by Richard Hamilton; illustrated by Sophy Williams p. cm.
Summary: Various animals eat up Polly's picnic but make it up to her later.
ISBN 1-58234-819-7 (alk. paper)
[1. Picnicking—Fiction. 2. Sharing—Fiction. 3. Animals--Fiction. 4. Stories in rhyme.]
I. Williams, Sophy, ill. II. Title.
PZ8.3.H1862 Po 2003   [E]—dc21   2002027823

First U.S. Edition 2003
1 3 5 7 9 10 8 6 4 2

Bloomsbury USA Children's Books
175 Fifth Avenue
New York, New York 10010

Polly's Picnic

by Richard Hamilton

illustrated by Sophy Williams

BLOOMSBURY
CHILDREN'S
BOOKS

When the sun shone brightly
in the clear blue sky and the
summer birds darted through the air —

Polly went for a picnic down by the river.

She lay in the sun, popped open her basket
and lazily started to dream . . .

Then —

Quack-Quack!
Attack!
Some ducks stole her snack
and gobbled it up
in midstream!

Polly opened up her sandwich box
and found beside her — Mr. Fox.

"Go on," she said. "Have one."
He did…and two…and three…and four.
He ate until there were no more.

She poured some milk into a cup
and — in a flash — two cats purred up.
Polly wasn't pleased but she could see
that they were hungrier than she.

"Have a sip," said Polly.
"It's awfully hot."
But those greedy cats
drank every drop!

"Hey!" cried Polly. "I'm thirsty too —
I didn't bring that milk for you."

Then, in her basket, she found a pear,
and suddenly, a horse was there.

"Have a bite," said Polly. "One bite. NO MORE."
But he ate it all — even the core!

Polly gasped,
Polly growled.
Polly very nearly howled!

"Can I have some?" asked a goat, emerging from the undergrowth.

Polly snapped, "The basket's empty." The goat replied, "That looks like plenty."

He opened his mouth,
he licked his lips,
he chewed the basket into bits!

When the sun shone brightly
in the clear blue sky
and the summer birds
darted through the air —

Polly cried:
"It's just not fair.
I gave you my food
and drink for free

and now there's nothing left for me.
No one said thank you,
no one said please!
You've ruined my picnic under the trees!"

A swan gliding past heard her complain
and said to the ducks,
"You should be ashamed —
Polly's upset
because of your greed.
You must put this right
with all possible speed."

So the ducks
asked the fox,

and the fox
asked the cats.

The cats asked the horse.
The horse asked the goat.

"Who's been greedy?
Who's been rude?
Who has stolen
Polly's food?"

Jumping on the horse's back,
they galloped smartly up the track.

"There's Polly's house," the two cats cried.
They found the door and burst inside.

Then they measured, mixed and baked biscuits, sandwiches, sausages, cakes.

Back to the river they carried the food
on heads and tails, in paws and hooves.

There they found Polly, looking sad.
"We're sorry," they said. "We've been terribly bad."

Together they had a picnic with tea
and everybody shared
with everybody.

"Friends," said Polly, "I am no longer sad.
That's the best picnic I've ever had.

Thank you!"